Josephine Wants To Dance

Written by Jackie French

Illustrated by Bruce Whatley

First published in Australia by HarperCollins*Publishers* Pty Limited in 2006
First published in paperback in Great Britain by HarperCollins Children's Books in 2008

10 9 8 7 6 5 4 3 2 1
ISBN-13: 978-0-00-726316-5
ISBN-10: 0-00-726316-3

Text copyright © Jackie French 2006
Illustrations copyright © Farmhouse Illustration Company Pty Limited 2006

HarperCollins Children's Books is a division of HarperCollins Publishers Ltd.

Visit our website at: www.harpercollinschildrensbooks.co.uk

Bruce Whatley used acrylic paints to create the illustrations for this book.

Printed and bound by Printing Express, Hong Kong

To Fuchsia, the roo who danced around our lives,
and to Bruce, who turns words into magic. JF

To my new friend Phoebe R, who loves to line dance. BW

Josephine loved to dance.

She bounced with the brolgas ...

and leapt with the lyrebirds.

'Kangaroos don't dance,
Josephine!'
said her little brother Joey.
'They hop.'

But Josephine took no notice.

The emus showed her how to point her toes.
The eagles taught her how to soar
to the music of the wind.

Josephine whirled like the clouds across the gully.
She swayed with the branches in the trees.

But still she dreamt of
somehow finding another
way to dance.

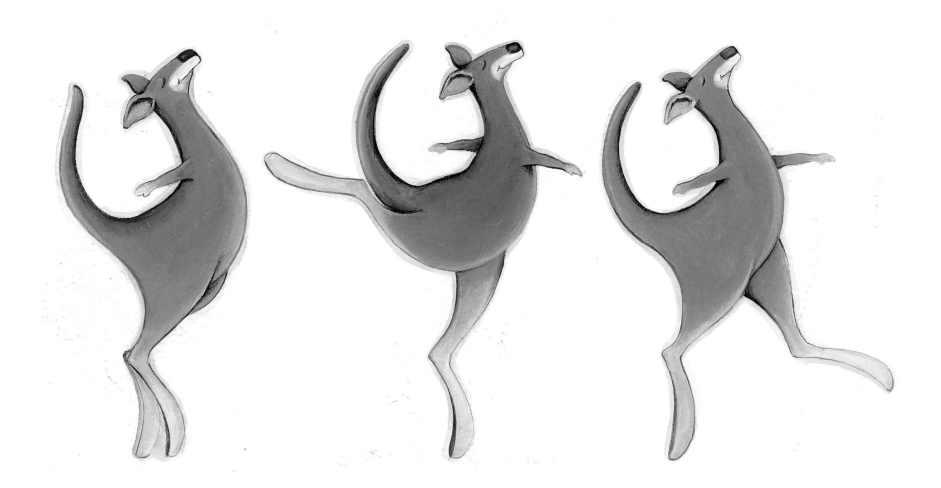

'There has to be something more!'
said Josephine wistfully as she danced
across her brother.

'Kangaroos don't
dance, Josephine!'
yelled Joey, ducking his head.
'They jump.'

But Josephine kept
on dancing.

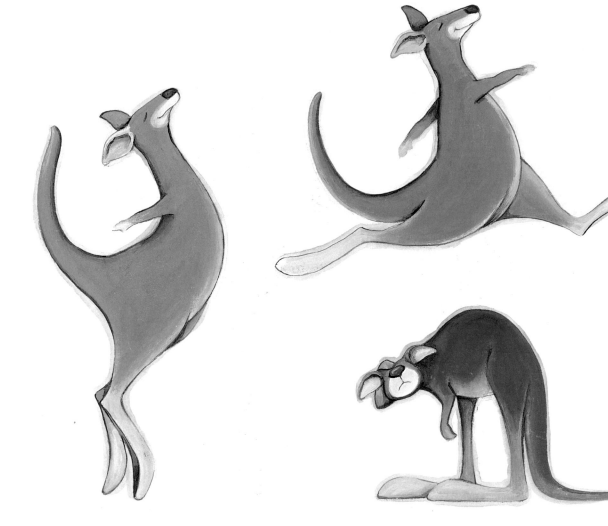
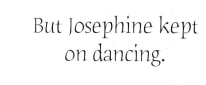
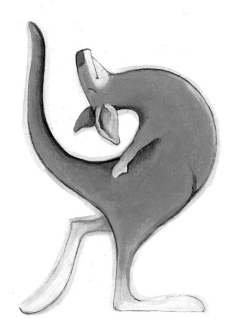

The next day Josephine found
posters stuck on the trees. The ballet
was coming to Shaggy Gully!

'That's how I'd like to dance!'
cried Josephine. 'In a pink tutu,
with silk ballet shoes.'

'Get real!' said Joey.
'Kangaroos don't wear tutus, Josephine!
And they never wear silk ballet shoes.'

'I'm going to,' said Josephine,
pointing her toes.

She crept over to the hall …

and peered through
the window as the
dancers rehearsed.

A week later Josephine
sneaked into town.

'Ohhh!' cried Josephine.

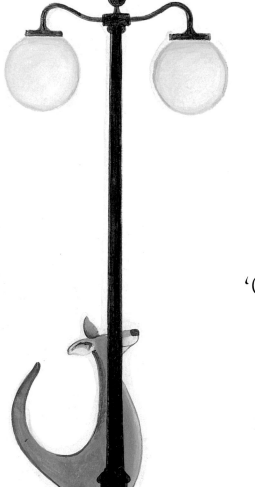

She watched the dancers for hours.
Then she practised at night … all alone.

She spun, she swirled, she pirouetted …
and at the end she always curtsied.

'I really **am** becoming a dancer now,'
thought Josephine.

The day of the first
performance arrived.
But the ballet company
was in trouble!

'Ow!' shrieked the prima ballerina as she twisted her ankle.

'Ohhh!' sobbed the understudy as she found a splinter in her toe.

'Who will dance the lead role?'
cried the ballet director.

'Who else can leap so high?'

Josephine jumped ...

through the window ...
   and on to the stage.

'A kangaroo!' yelled the dancers.
'There's a kangaroo on the stage!'

Josephine pointed her toes. She tossed her head.
She swayed like the lyrebirds as they call to their sweethearts.
She soared like an eagle through the sky.

'A dancing kangaroo!' everyone cried.
'Who ever heard of a dancing kangaroo?'

Josephine swirled above the stage like the mist playing with the moon.

The director stared at Josephine.
Finally, she smiled. 'Well, this kangaroo
can dance — and she knows the lead role.
And she can jump higher than
any other dancer I've seen!'

The director took Josephine
to the wardrobe department.

'A kangaroo!' exclaimed the costume designer.

'I can't dress a kangaroo!'

'Just do your best,'
the director told him.

The costume designer quickly
altered a tutu for Josephine.

He stretched some ballet shoes too.
They were probably the longest
ballet shoes in the world.

At last it was time
for the performance.
The audience took their seats.
The orchestra tuned up.

Josephine stood backstage,
waiting for the music to begin.

'Josephine!' hissed Joey
through the window.
'What are you doing?
Come back to the bush
at once!'

'No!' said Josephine.
'I'm going to dance. In a pink
tutu, with silk ballet shoes.
I'm going to jump higher than any
other dancer in the world!'

The lights dimmed.
The orchestra started playing.
The curtains opened.
The performance began.

The ballerinas fluttered on to the stage ...   one ...   two ...   three ...

four ...   and ...   Josephine!

Someone in the audience giggled. 'It's a kangaroo!'

Then Josephine began to dance.

She twirled through the air like leaves in a whirlwind.
She leapt like no dancer ever had before.
And at the end she curtsied like the brolgas bowing to the sun.

The audience were silent.

And then they clapped.

And then they ...

cheered!

'This kangaroo is a dancer!' they cried.

'A truly magnificent dancer!'

Josephine was still curtsying
when the ballet director brought
bunches of roses on to the stage.

'Roses are delicious!' decided Josephine.

'And I am finally a dancer – and it's fun!'

In fact, dancing
looked like so much
fun that soon all
the audience …

were bounding and bouncing...

and prancing and pouncing...

bumping and jumping...

and leaping and thumping ...

swishing and swirling ...

and twinkle-toe twirling ...

but nobody **ever** danced quite like ...

josephine!